To Scout and Poppy

This paperback edition first published in 2021 by Andersen Press Ltd.
First published in Great Britain in 2020 by Andersen Press Ltd.,
20 Vauxhall Bridge Road, London SW1V 2SA.
Copyright © Michael Foreman, 2020.
The right of Michael Foreman to be identified as the
author and illustrator of this work has been asserted by him
in accordance with the Copyright, Designs and Patents Act, 1988.
All rights reserved.
Colour separated in Switzerland by Photolitho AG, Zürich.
Printed and bound in Malaysia.

1   3   5   7   9   10   8   6   4   2

British Library Cataloguing in Publication Data available.
ISBN 978 1 78344 859 3

This book belongs to:

_____

I DIDN'T DO IT!

MICHAEL FOREMAN

ANDERSEN PRESS

Milo loves his new bike.

One day, he hopes to be a champion racer.

Today, Milo is in a hurry,
the Big Cycle Race is coming to town
and he doesn't want to miss it!

WHOOOOOSH!

He can hear the crowd cheering.

QUICK! QUICK!

The cheering is getting louder and **louder**.

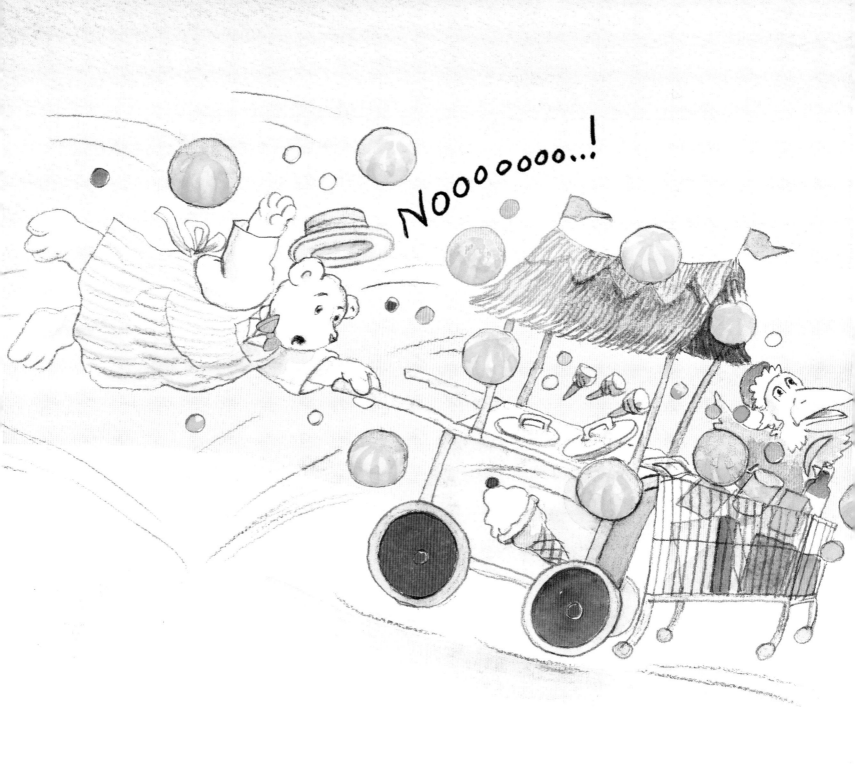

The racers are getting closer...

And here they are!

But Milo wants to see the finish!

The finish is in sight...

WHEEEEEEEEEE!

I DIDN'T DO IT!

QUICK! QUICK!

Here it is, the finishing line...

but who will take the prize?

Oh, no! Not him! STOP THIEF!

Catch him, somebody!

And somebody CATCH THE BABY!

Hooray for Milo,

HE DID IT!

Other books by Michael Foreman:

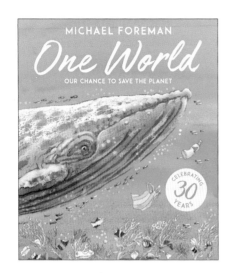

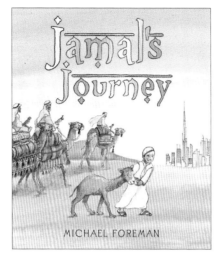

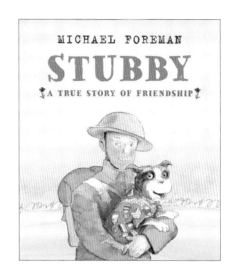

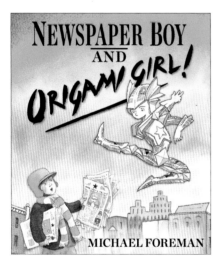

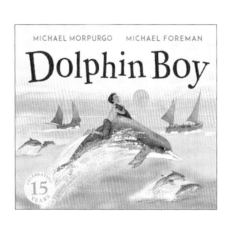